THE ENORMOUS POTATO

To my mother, Edith Cohen — A.D.

In memory of my mother and father, who first told me this tale many years ago — D.P.

First U.S. edition 1998

Text © 1997 Aubrey Davis
Illustrations and hand lettering © 1997 Dušan Petričić

Kids Can Press gratefully acknowledges the financial support of the Government
of Ontario, through the Ontario Media Development Corporation; the Ontario
Arts Council; the Canada Council for the Arts; and the Government of Canada,
through the CBF, for our publishing activity.

Published in Canada and the U.S. by Kids Can Press Ltd.
25 Dockside Drive, Toronto, ON M5A 0B5

Kids Can Press is a Corus Entertainment Inc. company

www.kidscanpress.com

The artwork in this book was rendered in watercolor and pencil
on 140 lb Bockingford watercolor paper.
The text is set in Bodoni.

Printed and bound in Buji, Shenzhen, China, in 5/2018 by WKT Company

CM 97 0 9 8 7 6 5
CM PA 99 20 19 18

Library and Archives Canada Cataloguing in Publication

Davis, Aubrey
        The enormous potato

ISBN 978-1-55074-386-9 (bound)   ISBN 978-1-55074-669-3 (pbk.)

I. Petričić, Dušan.   II. Title.

PS8557.A832E56 1997   jC813'.54   C97-930196-3
PZ7.D38En 1997

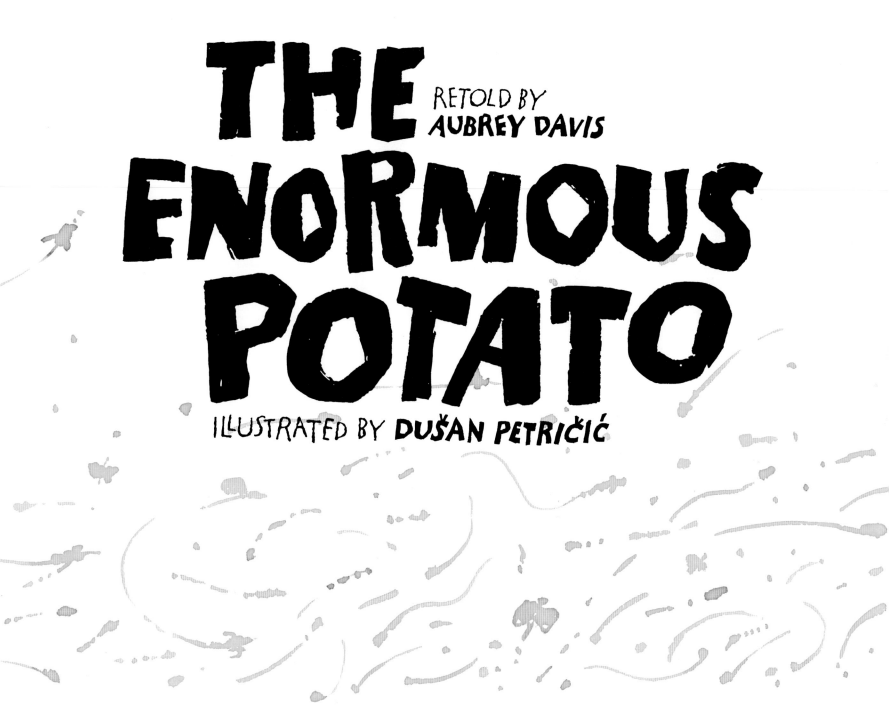

THE ENORMOUS POTATO

RETOLD BY **AUBREY DAVIS**

ILLUSTRATED BY **DUŠAN PETRIČIĆ**

KIDS CAN PRESS

There once was a farmer who had an eye.
It wasn't like your eye or my eye.
It was a potato eye.
The farmer planted it.
And it grew into a potato.

The potato grew bigger and bigger.

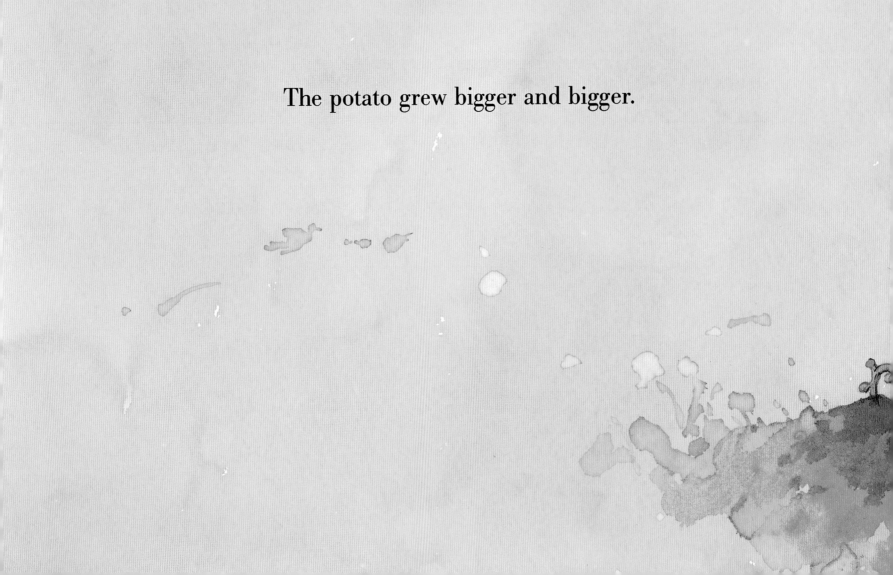

It grew fat.
It grew enormous.

It was the biggest potato
in the world.

"It's time to pull it out,"
said the farmer.
So he grabbed the potato.
He pulled and pulled again.
But the potato wouldn't
come out of the ground.
So he called his wife.

The wife grabbed the farmer.
The farmer grabbed the potato.
They pulled and pulled again.
But the potato wouldn't
come out of the ground.
So the wife called their daughter.

The daughter grabbed the wife.
The wife grabbed the farmer.
The farmer grabbed the potato.
They pulled and pulled again.
But the potato wouldn't
come out of the ground.
So the daughter called the dog.

"ROWF! ROWF! ROWF!"

The dog grabbed the daughter.
The daughter grabbed the wife.
The wife grabbed the farmer.
The farmer grabbed the potato.
They pulled and pulled again.
But the potato wouldn't
come out of the ground.
So the dog called the cat.

"MEOW! MEOW! MEOW!"

The cat grabbed the dog.

The dog grabbed the daughter.

The daughter grabbed the wife.

The wife grabbed the farmer.

The farmer grabbed the potato.

They pulled and pulled again.

But the potato wouldn't

come out of the ground.

So the cat called the mouse.

"SQUEAK! SQUEAK! SQUEAK!"
The mouse grabbed the cat.
The cat grabbed the dog.
The dog grabbed the daughter.
The daughter grabbed the wife.
The wife grabbed the farmer.
The farmer grabbed the potato.
They pulled and pulled again.

RRRRRRRRRRRRRRRRRRRRRRRR...RIP!

Out came the potato!

"That's a big potato!"
said the farmer.
"That's a big potato!"
said the wife.
"That's a dirty potato!"
said the daughter.
So they washed it,
     and chopped it,
          and cooked it, too.

The smell of potato brought the people from town.

They brought forks.

They brought bowls.

They brought butter and salt.

Soon everyone was eating potato.

My, it was good.

They ate and they ate . . .

till the potato was gone.

And now the story is gone, too.